Wizard at Work

Other Books by Vivian Vande Velde

Wizard at Work

a novel in stories

VIVIAN VANDE VELDE

Harcourt, Inc.

Orlando   Austin   New York   San Diego   Toronto   London

www.HarcourtBooks.com

Library of Congress Cataloging-in-Publication Data
Vande Velde, Vivian.
Wizard at work/by Vivian Vande Velde.
p. cm.
Summary: A young wizard, who runs a school to teach wizards, looks forward to a quiet summer off but is drawn into adventures with princesses, unicorns, and ghosts instead.
[1. Wizards—Fiction. 2. Magic—Fiction.
3. Princesses—Fiction. 4. Humorous stories.] I. Title.
PZ7.V2773Wi 2003
[Fic]—dc21 2002068665
ISBN 0-15-204559-7

Text set in Stempel Garamond
Designed by Cathy Riggs

First edition
A C E G H F D B

Printed in the United States of America

To Gloria,
the word wizard

Contents

Wizard
at Work

How It All Starts

The wizard was minding his own business—well, mostly—when the witch either put a hex on him or didn't.

It happened like this: The wizard was a young man who often magically disguised himself to look like an old man because that was how people expected a wizard to look. Because he ran a school for young wizards, he spent the school year looking like an old man, for he figured he'd get little respect from his students if they guessed he was only a bit older than they. So once school was over for the year, it was a relief to take off his magical disguise and relax—sort of like taking off shoes that are too tight and fancy clothes that you've been worried about catching on something or spilling something on.

After what seemed an exceptionally harsh winter and a spring that surely had taken longer than usual to arrive, he had packed the last of his students off for home. On this, the first day of summer vacation, he magically transported himself to the village of Saint Wayne the Stutterer. Saint Wayne was not one of the major saints, and the village was a small one. The wizard knew most of the people there, and most of them knew him in his true form. He needed to buy supplies for his garden, including a new hoe, and he was waiting in line at the blacksmith's shop when the witch—whom he did not know—suddenly appeared with her three children.

Magically appeared.

As in: One moment, not there—the next, there.

Appeared directly in front of him about five seconds before the blacksmith finished with the previous customer, looked up, and asked, "Who's next?"

"That would be me," the witch said, stepping up to the counter.

The wizard was willing to give the woman the benefit of the doubt, to believe that she had magically transported herself to where she wanted to be, and that she hadn't intentionally cut in front of him. He was even willing to let her get waited on first, for he was in no rush. He was ready for warm, leisurely days of peace and quiet.

The witch's children, two boys and a girl, were poking, bumping, taunting, and teasing one another. The older boy was a bully, the younger boy was a sniveler, and the girl was a whiner. All three of the children called "Ma!" in shrill, annoying, insistent voices—as in, "Ma, he's doing it again!" and "Ma, she started it!" and "Ma, aren't you through here yet?"

The witch ignored them while she explained to the blacksmith about the gate latch she wanted repaired.

The wizard didn't have children of his own,

but he thought that having students was almost like having children. He thought to himself, *I would never let my children misbehave like this.* Of course, the youngest of his students was twelve, and the oldest of these children was seven, but that was no excuse.

The older boy knocked the younger boy backward so that he stepped on the wizard's toes.

"Careful," the wizard said, putting his hand on the boy's shoulder, for the boy gave no sign of recognizing that he wasn't, in fact, standing on the simple ground anymore.

The boy glanced over his shoulder to give the wizard a well-what-are-your-feet-doing-under-my-feet? look, and his brother took the opportunity to smack him on the back of the head. "Ma!" the younger boy sniveled, elbowing his sister for good measure.

"Ma," the girl whined.

"Ma!" the older boy said as though he were the victim.

The blacksmith was working on the latch, and the witch turned and glared at the wizard.

"*What?*" she asked, somewhere between a snarl and a snap.

The wizard wasn't willing to get into a fight, so he just shook his head to indicate he had nothing to say, and he inspected that part of the smithy where the ceiling met the back wall.

The witch glowered for a long moment before returning her attention to the blacksmith.

The children got louder and louder.

The witch didn't seem to hear them.

She did, however, hear the wizard sigh.

She turned around a second time and asked, "Do you have a problem with my children?"

"No," he assured her. He couldn't resist asking, "Do you?"

"How dare you?" she demanded. "How dare you criticize when you know nothing about us? Do you find my children annoying? Well, did you ever stop to consider whether there might be a reason for their misbehaving? Would you excuse them for being noisy and out of sorts if I told you they've been cooped up in the house for the past two weeks with illness? How about if I told you their father may not recover, and their little sister just died?"

"I'm so sorry," the wizard said, for though he had a tendency to get impatient quickly, he didn't wish ill on anyone. "I had no idea."

The witch snorted and turned back to the blacksmith, who had finished repairing the latch.

The wizard felt terrible for finding the family irksome when they'd been through so much hardship. Under the circumstances, he was willing to forgive them, even the little girl, who was sticking her tongue out at him.

The smaller boy was still sniveling, but now the wizard realized it was because he had a cold. He realized this when the boy, who had his finger stuck up his nose, withdrew that finger to wipe it on his brother's sleeve. The older boy didn't notice because he was surreptitiously tying his sister's braids together.

The witch paid the blacksmith, then said, "Come, children, now we're off to speak to the miller."

The wizard wanted her to know he regretted

looking down on her and her children, so he stood where he was and repeated, "I am truly sorry."

The witch was cross for his being in the way. "Why? What have you done now?"

"Nothing," he stammered. "I meant I'm sorry for all that's happened to you."

The witch glanced around suspiciously. "What happened?" she demanded.

The wizard was becoming confused. "The children's father, who's sick. The little girl who died."

"I never said there *was* sickness and death," the witch snarled as though he'd intentionally misunderstood. "I said, 'What if...' Actually, my children are the way they are because they're spoiled brats." She shook her head and pushed past him, muttering, "Dumb twit of a wizard." She added, "You'll never find true happiness until you learn to be less judgmental and look beyond the surface of things."

If that was a simple statement, it didn't really follow what she'd just said. If it was a spell, normally the wizard would have felt the magic, especially if it was being directed at him. But the children were jostling him as they pushed by on their way out, and he might have missed it.

Still, if it *was* a hex, it wasn't a bad one. He wasn't unhappy with his life as it was. He had his garden in the summer—when it wasn't overrun by rabbits—and fishing, and puttering about. And if he sometimes did get lonely, that was usually just about the time his students got back in the fall. Then, about the time they started really getting on his nerves, it would be summer again.

Life was satisfying, the wizard thought as he stepped up to the counter to give the blacksmith his order, if maybe somewhat predictable.

True happiness, he decided, was overrated.

The Beautiful Princess, the Wicked Stepmother, and the Ugly Stepsister

Once he got home, the wizard was happily tending his garden when a crow with a message tied to its leg came and refused to leave.

"Help," the message said. (It was written in lavender ink on pink stationery, all delicately perfumed and sealed with a miniature sealing-wax rose.) "I'm being held prisoner by my wicked stepmother, and my ugly stepsister has put a spell on both me and my betrothed. Please, please, *please*, help me."

It was signed, "Sincerely, Princess Rosalie," and whoever Princess Rosalie was, she had dotted the *i*'s in her name by drawing tiny roses.

The wizard could be cranky, but he had a soft spot in his heart for people in trouble, and this sounded like serious trouble. "How far?" he asked the crow.

The crow, standing on the left arm of the scarecrow in the wizard's garden, scratched at the ragged sleeve—twice.

Not two miles, that was for sure: The wizard knew everybody around here and there were no Princess Rosalies. "Two hours away?" he asked hopefully. He had a magic spell that could transport him at a moment's notice, but it only worked for places to which he had already been. Because he didn't know who or where this princess was, he would have to follow the crow she had sent. He'd need to walk—or go by horse. Horses, with their big yellow teeth and enormous, clumsy-looking feet, were not his favorite animal. "Is this princess two hours away?" he repeated.

The crow hopped to the scarecrow's head and pecked at one of the button eyes.

The wizard sighed. "Two days?"

The crow ruffled its feathers and took off in a northeasterly direction, then circled back and re-landed on the scarecrow's head.

The wizard sighed again. There was so much to do to get his garden in order. He tried to concentrate on the problems, on the reasons he shouldn't go—like the rabbits, who were no more intimidated by the scarecrow than this crow was, and who were making themselves at home in the wizard's garden. But he found himself looking at the pink-and-lavender note again. "Please, please, *please*, help me," he reread.

After yet another sigh, he muttered the spell that transformed his appearance into that of a man a hundred years older than he really was and that changed his practical work clothes into the star-sprinkled robe and conical hat he always wore in public, because otherwise nobody ever seemed to believe he really was a wizard.

He held his arm out for the crow, which landed on him with a flutter of black wings. Then it lifted its tail and made a mess on his sleeve.

"Bird brain," the wizard muttered.

But by then they were already transported to Farmer Seymour's barn, where there was a particularly bad-tempered mare that the farmer would rent out for an exorbitant fee whenever the wizard had need of a ride.

After two days of riding, the crow led the wizard to a small castle surrounded by a country town, all situated in the center of an especially green and peaceful valley.

And there, strolling down the wide avenue that led from the castle, was the wicked stepmother (he was sure it must be her) and the ugly stepsister.

The mother was a tall, thin woman dressed all in black. Her eyes, the wizard thought, were ferret-mean. And they were constantly moving—glancing this way and that—watching and evaluating all that went on around her.

Her daughter was a younger version of the same, except that her clothes were garishly colorful and she had a loud laugh that reminded the wizard of a pig oinking.

He did not want to make a formal entrance into the castle, for there was no telling how the wicked stepmother would react—wicked stepmothers can be unpredictable. Better to circle the castle and go in the back way. So with what he hoped looked like an expression of disinterested boredom, he rode by the group of townspeople that had gathered around the two women.

However, Princess Rosalie's messenger crow apparently did not reason the way the wizard did. Seeing him miss the turnoff to the castle, the crow rose up from its riding place on the horse's rump and began circling the wizard's head, cawing frantically.

"Shhh!" The wizard brushed his hand in front of his face to keep the frenzied bird at a safe distance.

It swooped at his head, pulling up only at the last moment with an angry screech. Then it climbed back into the air for another pass. And then another. And another.

People watched: The wicked queen and her daughter, passersby on the street, merchants at their outdoor stands—all stopped what they were doing to stare. A street juggler, distracted, dropped one of his clubs, then tucked them all under his red-and-green satin sleeve, unwilling to compete for the attention of the rapidly growing crowd.

"Stop it!" the wizard hissed at the crow.

He rounded his shoulders and slouched down into the saddle to make himself less conspicuous, but that only made the children in the crowd point and squeal, "Look at the hunchback and his trained bird!"

The wizard put his heels to the horse's sides, but the temperamental animal whipped around and nipped at him. Moving his leg farther back, out of range of the horse's big teeth, didn't help, for the horse kept after him, circling like a dog chasing its tail—or like the crow, still repeatedly diving at him. Finally he lifted both legs up and crossed them on top of the saddle.

The crowd clapped in polite appreciation.

The wizard pulled off his hat and swung at the crow, using the hat as a net. He almost fell off the horse. Not until his fourth try did he catch the crow. He quickly moved his hand to close off the top of the hat.

The crowd cheered. He heard someone thank the queen for sending such fine entertainment on a market-day afternoon.

Holding the violently shaking hat away from him and ignoring the outraged squawking that came from it, the wizard did his best to smile calmly and sweetly, and he bowed to the appreciative audience. He sneaked a glance at the queen. She had her eyes narrowed to thin slits and had her eyebrows lowered ominously. Under his breath, the wizard whispered, "Move, you stupid horse."

By now he had gathered a loyal following of children, a regular parade. They tracked after him as he rode away from the castle. "Mister!" they kept insisting. "Hey, mister! What are you going to do with the bird next, mister?"

But finally, almost a mile beyond the last cottage of the town, his silence and the lack of further tricks from bird or horse got to them, and one by one the children fell away.

When the last child was out of sight, the wizard took hold of the tip of his hat and shook. The crow gave an angry squawk and shot off in the direction of the castle.

The wizard hurriedly said the spell that transformed himself into a bird.

Farmer Seymour's horse must have felt the tingle in the air that accompanies magic, for it whinnied and got that wild-eyed look it always did whenever it was seriously considering biting him. But by then the wizard was flying away toward the castle.

If I'm lucky, he thought, *the horse will run home before I get back.*

The wizard could keep a different shape for only a short while, but much sooner than that his shoulders began to ache from all the flapping. The crow he followed seemed to sense his distress and cruelly circled the castle twice before selecting a high tower window to fly into. With his last strength, the wizard landed on the windowsill, then transformed back into his own self so quickly that he almost fell backward off the sill.

Someone in the room screamed.

The wizard clutched the window frame and half jumped, half fell into the room.

It was a bedroom, a lady's bedroom; and although the time must have been about two o'clock in the afternoon, the young lady in question was in her bed. She clutched the sheets tight up around her neck, looking ready to scream again.

"Please don't do that," the wizard begged, clapping his hands over his ears. She was a very big lady—and she had an equally big voice.

To the wizard's surprise, the lady calmed down immediately. He could see her mouth move, but to form words, not to shriek.

"Beg your pardon?" he asked, slowly uncovering his ears.

She had raised the sheet up to hide the bottommost of her several chins. "I said, 'You're the wizard, aren't you?'" She didn't wait for his answer, but held the sheet up with one hand to block her face, and with her other hand pulled off her nightcap and fluffed her dark hair. She grabbed a mirror from the nightstand, and—still under cover of the sheet—started primping.

"Please don't bother," the wizard murmured. "I'm just passing through."

As if he hadn't spoken, she explained, "I didn't realize you'd be here so fast or I'd have made some arrangements."

"You see," the wizard continued as if *she* hadn't spoken, "I was following this crow. And it flew in here—you must have noticed it?" He spotted the vile creature, sitting on one of her bedposts, glowering. "And I didn't realize this was someone's room, and I'm terribly sorry, so I'll just be leaving now."

Still ignoring the wizard's words, the lady

went on, "I was thinking something along the order of a room divider or a screen for the first meeting, until I could explain."

"You see, I'm on an important mission…"

"But I suppose this will have to do, if you'll just give me another moment…"

"I have to rescue a princess—"

She emerged from under the sheet, smiling triumphantly and wearing a crown. "There."

"Princess Rosalie," he finished.

"Yes," she said, and gave a regal bow of the head.

The wizard, with his hand on the door, froze. He looked at the lady, who was almost as round as a ball, then he looked at the door, then at the lady again. He cleared his throat. "Princess Rosalie?" he repeated in a very small voice.

Her patience with him finally cracked. "If it's a shock to you, think how I feel," she snapped.

"I beg your pardon?"

"The *spell*, Wizard, my ugly stepsister's magic spell."

"Ah!"

Princess Rosalie picked up her mirror again. "Is it really that bad?" She glanced at her reflection, then wiped a tear from her eye.

"No," the wizard hurried to say. "No, really." She was huge, but her face was actually quite lovely. Somehow, he didn't think she'd appreciate his saying so.

Princess Rosalie reached around the brass headboard and banged the edge of her mirror against the wall. "Bernard!" she called. Then, to the wizard, "If you think I'm bad, wait until you see Prince Bernard."

Before he could think what answer he could possibly give to *that*, the wizard heard a scratching sound at the door.

"If you don't mind?" The princess motioned toward the door.

Slowly, warily, the wizard opened it, and a large Saint Bernard bounded in, knocking him down.

"Prince Bernard—Wizard," the princess said by way of introduction. "Wizard—Prince Bernard."

"Friendly fellow, at least," the wizard managed to say, as the dog sat on his chest and licked his face.

Princess Rosalie started to wail. Loudly.

As though to comfort her, Prince Bernard went over and began to lick her hand, but she snatched it away. "Look at him! And he drools. And he has fleas."

Unperturbed, the dog-prince sat down, his tail thumping against the floor.

"I see your problem." The wizard got back to his feet. "You say your stepsister did this?"

"Yes." Princess Rosalie pouted. "And now she and that hateful boyfriend of hers plot with my stepmother to keep me a prisoner here."

He was about to say that countering the magic of someone who did not want his or her magic countered was just about the hardest kind of spell—but that he would do his best—when he heard voices approaching.

Princess Rosalie heard them, too. She gasped, "They're coming! Quick, hide!"

The wizard glanced about the room hurriedly,

though Prince Bernard remained calm, scratching behind an ear.

"Hurry!" the princess cried.

The wizard pulled open the door of a large armoire, but it was so jammed with dresses, shoes, and plumed hats that there was no room for him or the dog.

"Oh, for goodness' sake!" Princess Rosalie threw back the covers and made to jump out of the bed. Instead, she floated—very slowly—to the ceiling. The wizard felt his jaw drop. The princess kicked the wall in frustration and went gracefully sailing in the opposite direction.

Prince Bernard raised his head and began to howl.

"What are you doing?" the wizard asked.

"It's more of that miserable spell!" Princess Rosalie cried. "My stepsister said, 'Let my sister become big and fat and swell up like a hot-air balloon'—that's exactly what she said. And now look at me."

The door flung open and the wicked-looking queen strode in, followed by her shifty-eyed daughter. "Rosalie, we heard you scre—" The queen's eyes narrowed at the wizard, and her thin lips pursed, and for a moment he was afraid that—should she know magic, as her elder daughter evidently did—she would put a spell on him before he had a chance to react. But then her attention snapped back to her stepdaughter, who had just bumped into the dresser and knocked off all the combs and perfumes. "Rosalie! Get down from there at once before you hurt yourself."

With all the dignity she could muster, the floating princess said, "Would *some*body please?..."

The wizard took hold of her by the ankle and pulled her back down.

"Thank you." Princess Rosalie sat on the edge of the bed and daintily rearranged her dressing gown to make sure her knees were covered, but she held on to her ruffled pillow for ballast.

"Yes," the wicked queen said, turning back to the wizard, "thank you, kind sir." She squinted at him again. "Haven't I seen you somewhere before?"

"Oh," said Princess Rosalie, "no. I don't think so. This wizard just dropped by to offer to help find Prince Bernard. Didn't you, Wizard?"

The wizard looked at the ugly stepsister, who was scratching the head of the Saint Bernard—which did, as Princess Rosalie had mentioned earlier, show a tendency to drool. He looked at the wicked stepmother, who was still peering at him through narrowed eyes. It suddenly occurred to him that she was nearsighted, and that she squinted to see better. "I think," he said, "I think I need a hint before I can guess what's going on here. Are you two keeping Princess Rosalie a prisoner?"

"Poor Rosalie is the victim of a magical spell," the stepsister explained, and despite her ugly, mean-looking face, her voice was sad and full of concern.

"Not yours?"

The stepsister was too surprised to answer. Her mouth opened and closed twice, before she finally shook her head.

"Hers," the queen said. And pointed to Princess Rosalie herself.

"I think I'm getting a headache," the huge princess said. "Maybe you'd all better leave now."

"What have you been telling this man?" the queen asked, though not unkindly.

Princess Rosalie squirmed.

"You see," the stepsister said, "Francis—he's the Master Craftsman of the Wood-Carvers Guild—Francis has been sort of courting me, and he gave us this nice fat goose for dinner last week."

The wizard didn't see what that had to do with anything, but he gave her the benefit of the doubt and nodded for her to go on.

"He had gotten it from this little old lady who lives in a cottage near the town wall, and she's always claimed to be a witch, but we never took that seriously—she's always been a bit odd, but so are a lot of other people—but, anyway, she gave him the goose in payment for a chair he had made for her, and he brought it here—the goose, not the chair—and we had it for dinner, because even though she said it was a magic goose, she says lots of things, but then after dinner we found the wishbone, and Rosalie and I decided to make a wish, so I took one end, and she took the other, and we both pulled—"

"Yes," the wizard urged, his patience beginning to wear. "And?"

"—and, it broke right down the center, so I thought that meant we'd each get our wish, but Rosalie said it meant neither of us would, and when we asked the little old lady, she said, 'That means you each get the other's wish.'"

"Ah! Switched wishes." He turned to Princess Rosalie. "Is this true?"

Again the princess squirmed, but he wouldn't stop looking at her. "Well...," she said. And still he stared. "More or less." And *still* he stared. "Yes!" she shouted.

Let my sister become big and fat and swell up like a hot-air balloon. Rosalie had claimed that this was what her stepsister had said. It must have been what she herself had wished. She must have added, *And let her boyfriend turn into a dog, too.* But for the moment the wizard was more curious about something else. He turned to the stepsister. "What did you wish for?"

She looked embarrassed, but explained, "Well, you see, even though Rosalie has always been very beautiful, and talented, and popular, she was sad, and she was always saying she wished for this, or she wished for that, so even though we don't get along all that well, I felt sorry for her, so I wished she'd have health and love and happiness, which I figured are the most important things in the world, and because the wish by its very nature has to be secret, and because I didn't know what she was wishing for—"

"And did you get the benefit of that wish yourself?" the wizard interrupted.

She blushed, right up to her beady little eyes. "Well, Francis—he's the Master Craftsman of the Wood-Carvers Guild—"

"Yes?"

"—Francis is leading the search party that's looking for Prince Bernard—Prince Bernard is

Rosalie's betrothed, but he disappeared all of a sudden last week just at the same time all this trouble started—and we asked the little old lady who claims to be a witch, and she says she doesn't know anything about it and can't *do* anything about it, and Francis is looking all over to find him because we're so afraid he's been hurt or lost, but I'm sure they'll find him and he'll be all right, and then after they get back, Francis has asked that he and I get married, which I'd been hoping he'd ask for a long time, and I said yes."

This was quite a mouthful, even for her, and she finally had to stop to take a breath. The wizard looked at the Saint Bernard, which was scratching itself again. Princess Rosalie made a strangled whimpering sound, and the wizard took pity on her. "Well, because it's just a wishbone spell, it'll be easy enough for me to break."

Princess Rosalie and her stepmother and her stepsister all sighed in relief.

"And as for Prince Bernard, I can help there, too. So why don't you contact Francis"—he couldn't resist adding—"the Master Craftsman of the Wood-Carvers Guild, and tell him to come on home."

"Oh, thank you!" The mean-faced stepsister threw her arms around him and kissed his cheek, while her mother curtsied to him.

"Best of luck to both of you always," he added, as they started to leave. And if they noticed the spell-casting flip of his wrist or heard the strange, formal words that accompanied it, they didn't say.

Before the door had even clicked shut, the wizard made a big wave with his arms and said some more magic words.

The huge princess, sitting so lightly on the edge of her bed, diminished to about a quarter of her former size and sank solidly into her down mattress.

The Saint Bernard, sitting on the floor by her feet with his tongue hanging out, tipped and fell over. Before he hit the floor, he had turned back into a young man. "I say," the prince said, scratching his head. And then again, "I say." He had a vacant, amiable look that had been more becoming when his face had been that of a dog. But the wizard figured that was Princess Rosalie's problem.

Without a word to them, he started the gesture and incantation to transport himself back home. But then he stopped, just long enough to point a warning finger at the princess. "I hope you learned your lesson," he said.

And he was already home by the time he added, very softly, "*I* certainly did."

Beasts
on the Rampage

In the pond beyond his garden, the wizard was in his rowboat, which was held together more by spells than patches—because, long as July days are, they never seemed long enough both to fix the old fishing boat and to fish. Whenever it came down to making a decision, fixing or fishing, he always leaned more toward fishing.

On the off chance that the warmth of the midsummer sun and the gentle swaying of the boat might, by coincidence, make him doze off, he had brought a pillow. He had his straw hat over his face—strictly to prevent sunburn—and he was just thinking that the last thing he needed at this perfect moment was for a fish to actually bite on the end of his line, when he heard someone call, "Halllloooo!"

No, the wizard suddenly realized, *a visitor* was the last thing he needed.

Maybe, he thought, this was just a case of a sound carrying over the stillness of the day. Maybe whoever was calling was, in fact, calling someone else.

"Halllooo, Wizard!" the voice hailed.

Drat! the wizard thought. He considered pretending he was asleep, but he suspected this person would not be deterred and would just keep on yelling until he became a real irritant.

Or I could pretend I haven't heard, the wizard thought, *and row for the farther shore.* But the pond wasn't that big. If the wizard rowed to the other side, whoever this was could walk around and meet him there.

The wizard considered doing a transporting spell, but that was silly: running away from his own home to avoid an unwanted visitor. And where would he go? And how long would he have to stay away to discourage this man into leaving?

With a sigh, the wizard sat up, placed the hat back on the top of his head, and began rowing to shore. *Maybe this won't take too long,* he told himself. He kept his own, true appearance, hoping his youthfulness would discourage the man. But his visitor was young himself, and not easily discouraged.

He tried to help the wizard out of the boat, though the wizard was perfectly capable and used to doing it on his own, so that they both ended up ankle-deep in a muddy patch on the bank.

"I'm so glad I found you at home," the man chattered at him. "I come from the village of Saint Wayne the Stutterer, and we need your help."

At least Saint Wayne the Stutterer was close by, just on the other side of the hill. The wizard dared to hope this might be quick after all.

"What's the problem?" he asked.

"Wild beasts on the rampage," the man said.

"What kind of beasts?" The wizard was

thinking, *Rabid wolves?* Diseased wolves, unlike healthy wolves, would attack people. *Wild boar?* The villagers had recently cleared a section of the forest, and maybe, with their territory destroyed, a family of boar—always aggressive animals— had turned on them. *A pack of feral dogs? Dragons? Basilisks?*

The man from Saint Wayne's said, "Unicorns."

The wizard shuddered. He said, "I'll go there immediately."

The mayor of Saint Wayne the Stutterer was a woman named Enid, who had been voted into the top position when her husband, the previous mayor, had run off with the town treasury. Enid was a large woman who was honest and forthright and had a lot of common sense—attributes her missing husband didn't share.

The wizard transported himself to the village and found Enid in her kitchen, kneading and pounding bread dough. Without a town treasury, there was no way to pay the mayor a salary, so Enid had to support herself.

"Hello, Wizard," Enid said, pausing in her work. "Thanks for coming so quickly."

"I know how unicorns can be," the wizard said. "Are these mature unicorns gone bad, or yearlings?"

"Yearlings," Enid said, picking pieces of dough off the backs of her hands, "about a half dozen of them. Adolescent males showing off for the females, tough females—the kind that wear their manes all spiked and that laugh and egg the males on. They all get drunk eating fermented fruit, then come into town, where they make faces at the little kids, chew tobacco and spit it out on the sidewalk, form crop circles with the power of their horns, kick mud on the farm horses and call them 'no-horns.' We hoped they would move on, but the trouble's been escalating: They walk all in a line, intimidating people into getting out of their way. Goosing old folks with their horns. Breaking windows, though always at night—there's never any proof. Things disappear off laundry lines. But last night…"

Enid paused and the wizard could guess what

she was going to say next. All of this was following a typical pattern.

"Last night," she continued, "they broke into Farmer Seymour's barn, grabbed one of the pigs, and had a pig roast out on the beach."

The wizard shook his head. "Unicorns that eat meat only get wilder."

"That's why we sent for you."

"Any idea where they're likely to be?" the wizard asked.

"Well, that's another thing," Enid told him. "My son, Jack, has been hanging around with them. That's another one that doesn't seem to have the sense he was born with. Don't get me started."

The wizard shook his head to indicate that getting her started was the last thing on his mind.

"I try to give Jack responsibilities, hoping to make him more mature, think things through, act like a rational person rather than like his father." She repeated, "Don't get me started."

The wizard guessed, "So...you're saying Jack's likely to be with the unicorns?"

"Try the pool hall," Enid suggested. "That's as

good a place as any to waste away a fine summer day."

"Thank you," the wizard said, backing out of her kitchen before she got started talking about sixteen-year-old sons or missing husbands or hooligan unicorns again.

Jack was in the pool hall, though the unicorns weren't. The wizard hadn't really thought they would be. Magical creatures or not, unicorns were at a definite disadvantage when it came to holding pool cues, and the management had a sign up saying:

> NO STRIKING BALLS
> WITH ANY OBJECTS
> EXCEPT DESIGNATED POOL CUES.

Jack was sitting at one of the tables in the bar area, his head pillowed by his arms. The wizard thought maybe the unicorns weren't the only ones overdoing the fermented fruit.

The wizard knew the smartest thing would be to ignore Jack and ask around to see if anybody else knew where the unicorns might be, but the young man was so obviously depressed, the wizard felt sorry for him. He went and sat down next to him.

"My mother," Jack said, without bothering to look up, "is going to kill me."

The wizard considered this statement. "Well, it's always a possibility, I suppose. But all in all, rather unlikely."

"No," Jack insisted. "My mother is going to kill me."

"Does this have anything to do with the unicorns?" the wizard asked, thinking they might have dared or taunted him into doing something he shouldn't have.

"I don't think so." Jack sat up and looked at the wizard. "Do unicorns cheat at cards?"

"Probably not," the wizard answered. "It's hard to have an ace up your sleeve when you don't, in fact, *have* a sleeve."

Jack gave the wizard a disgusted look. "I wasn't

playing cards with the unicorns. I was playing with a bunch of guys. You're the one who brought up the unicorns. I thought you were saying the unicorns sent those guys to win all my money from me." Jack winced. "Actually, it was my mother's money. She should never have trusted me. It's all her fault. Besides, I think the guys were cheating."

"What makes you say that?" the wizard asked.

Jack got that this-wizard-is-an-idiot look again and said, "Because they won all my money."

The wizard didn't point out that maybe they were just better cardplayers. Jack seemed to be the sort who liked to blame other people for his troubles.

Jack asked, "Do you think my mother would believe me if I told her I was robbed at knife-point?"

"As mayor," the wizard pointed out, "she'd feel responsible for protecting the village from armed bandits, so she'd have to investigate a report like that."

"How about a freak windstorm?" Jack asked.

"Freak windstorms aren't a mayor's responsibility. I could say the money was whipped out of my hand before I could put it safely away."

"You could tell the truth," the wizard suggested.

"I could," Jack mused. "Or, how about: I came across a poor, starving, diseased orphan child and I thought, 'We have so much more than he does,' so I gave the money away?"

The wizard would have left Jack to remain there feeling sorry for himself, but he hated to inflict the lad on Enid. "Maybe if you helped me find and control the unicorns, your mother would forgive you."

"What would you pay me?" Jack asked.

"Nothing," the wizard said.

"Oh, well, that's not such a wonderful deal, then," Jack said.

I definitely should have left him alone and asked somebody else, the wizard thought, getting to his feet.

But Jack got up also. "All right, I'll help you," he said. "Maybe if I get killed, then my mother will forgive me."

The unicorns, Jack told the wizard, were probably in Farmer Seymour's north field. They liked to bother Farmer Seymour because his face turned such an interesting shade of purple when he got angry.

As the wizard and Jack approached the north field, they could smell the enticing aroma of roasting meat.

"Uh-oh," Jack said. "Smells like they got another of Farmer Seymour's pigs."

The wizard sniffed. *Not pork,* he decided. *Beef.* The unicorns were behaving worse and worse. Unstopped, they would develop a craving for dragon meat. The dragons would be understandably irritated and would wage war on the unicorns—dragon flame against unicorn magic. That would be the end of any farmland—or farmer—caught between the two factions.

And the worst unicorns eventually went after the most challenging game of all: humans.

But for the moment, these unicorns had turned their attention to Farmer Seymour's shed, which had an easy-to-climb-onto roof. The males were taking turns daring one another to jump off it to impress the females.

As Jack and the wizard got to the pit where the unicorns were roasting their cow, all six unicorns stepped in front of the fire as though worried that the wizard would try to take their carnivore-style meal away from them. They started to whistle and jeer. "Hey, Jack," they called out, "who's your *old* friend?"

And the wizard didn't even have his old-man disguise on.

The wizard was relieved to see that Enid had been right: These were immature unicorns. They would probably settle down with age, if they didn't provoke interspecies war before then.

The wizard told them, "Why don't you go home and leave the people of this village alone? Surely your parents are missing you."

"Surely nobody's missing *you*," one of the unicorns sneered. The other unicorns laughed as though this were incredibly clever.

If the wizard had known where the parents of

these unicorns were, he could have used his transporting spell to send them there. The parents would no doubt be able to tell exactly how much fermented fruit their offspring had been consuming, and the wizard doubted these unicorns would be allowed out unsupervised for a good long time.

But because the wizard *didn't* know where the parents were, that wouldn't work.

He could simply transport them away from the village of Saint Wayne the Stutterer, but that would just be passing the problem on to someone else.

"Why don't you use your energy to do something good?" he suggested.

"Oh, sure," one of the females said in a singsong voice. "Let's all go and pick some pretty flowers." She gave such a braying laugh that the wizard wondered if she realized she sounded just like a donkey.

"Jack, your friend is boring," the unicorns said. "Come and eat some roast cow with us."

Jack looked ready to join them, but he stopped when he saw a harness on the ground with a name painted on it.

"Bessie!" he cried.

"Uh-oh," one of the unicorns said, picking his teeth with the point of a rib bone, "another friend of yours?"

"Bessie was our cow!" Jack cried. "I just sold her at the market this morning."

"Uh-oh," the unicorn repeated. "We just stole her from the market this afternoon. Want her back?" He offered the rib bone to Jack "Some assembly required."

"Enough of this," the wizard commanded. "Go home now or I'll be forced to take drastic measures."

"Like what?" another of the unicorns demanded. "Make an ugly face like this?" He tipped his head back, bugged his eyes, dilated his nostrils, and stuck his tongue out.

"Oooo," the other five cried, "we're scared!"

Reason would get him nowhere, the wizard realized. He flung a spell at the adolescent unicorns to make them grow up and be more mature.

The unicorns, being magical creatures, felt the tingle of magic the moment it left the wizard's fingertips, and the two most alert instantly wove an enchanted barrier to protect all six of them from the wizard.

Spell hit counterspell not a handspan from the unicorns' noses, and a shower of silvery stars fell like dying fireworks onto the farmer's field.

The wizard cast the spell again, this time high up in the air, so that it would come down on the unicorns' heads, but the same two raised the shield above their group, and a third—not knowing what, exactly, the wizard's spell was meant to do—let healing energy pour out from her horn.

This time golden fireworks stars drifted toward the ground.

"Jack," the wizard muttered out of the side of his mouth, "distract them."

"Ahmmm," Jack said. "Look out behind you, unicorns. Here comes Farmer Seymour."

"How dumb do you think we are?" the unicorns asked.

The wizard cast a spell beyond the unicorns onto the fire that was roasting the unfortunate Bessie. He caused the fire to take the shape of Farmer Seymour, and he caused the crackling of the flames to sound like Farmer Seymour's voice. The voice seemed to say, "I don't know how dumb you are, but I'd guess *very.*"

Startled, the unicorns turned around, and the wizard hit them again with his spell to make them instantly grow a year older.

In the blink of a moment, they grew just a bit taller and lost the last traces of baby-fat roundness. They stood tall and proud rather than slouching.

One of the female unicorns said to the males, "You guys are, like, so immature."

"Actually," one of the males said in a new, deeper voice, "not anymore."

Another of the females said, "This meat thing freaks me out."

"Me, too," another of the males said. "Like, what have we got to prove to each other?"

Everybody agreed that they had nothing to prove, and that it was very irresponsible of them to be away from their families without having said where they were going, and that the adult thing to do would be to go home. "Good-bye, Jack," they called as they left. "Sorry about your cow and all."

The wizard went to that spot in the field where the three magics had met: wizardly *grow-up* spell, unicorn *shield* spell, and unicorn *healing* spell. Almost all of the golden stars had fizzled out before actually hitting the ground, but there was a slight sparkle on the grass that indicated some residual magic had taken physical form.

The wizard picked up the sparkling bits. There were three of them, each one smooth and no bigger than a bean.

"Can I have those?" Jack asked. "For helping you?"

But the magic must have been evaporating, for the golden sparkle disappeared, leaving three small, dirt-brown something-or-others in the wizard's palm.

"Oh," Jack said. "Never mind."

The wizard doubted there was any more magic in them at all, but he stuck the objects in his pocket just in case and headed back toward the village.

Jack ran to catch up. "I can't even bring the beef home to my mother—it's all burnt. She is absolutely going to kill me. Do you think she'd believe me if I told her the unicorns stole Bessie from me before I had a chance to sell her at the market, and that's why I don't have any money?"

The wizard considered casting a *grow-up* spell on Jack, but that was more dangerous with people than with animals. Besides, Enid might take it amiss if Jack came home suddenly having to shave every day.

"Have you ever considered telling the truth?" the wizard said. "Admit your mistake? Apologize? And determine that you'll never act so foolishly again? I think that if your mother saw you'd learned a lesson, she'd be willing to forgive you."

"I suppose," Jack agreed sullenly. But then he seemed to cheer up. He put his arm around the wizard's shoulder. "You know," he said, "that's good advice. I'm indebted to you."

The wizard was surprised and gratified that his words had had such a deep effect on the lad, and he carried that good feeling all the way back to Mayor Enid's house, where he found Enid in the yard, shaking out the kitchen rug.

"The unicorns have gone home," the wizard told her. Then, because Jack had had such a change of heart, he added, "Jack helped me."

"Thank you," Enid said to the wizard. And to Jack she remarked, "That's a surprise." Then she asked him, "Did you get a good price for the cow?"

"Well, it's an interesting thing about the cow...," Jack said as he led his mother inside.

The wizard lingered for a moment, hoping to hear Enid's reaction to Jack's confession, hoping he'd given Jack the right advice.

From inside the house, Enid's voice rose in indignant anger. "Magic beans?" she cried. "Magic beans? What in the world are you talking about— magic beans in exchange for a cow?"

The wizard clapped his hand to his pocket and found it empty. *Jack picked my pocket!* he thought crossly.

Three tiny objects came flying out of the kitchen window, narrowly missing the wizard's head. For a moment, they seemed to glitter, but the wizard convinced himself that it was just an optical illusion, the effect of the setting sun.

He could have scrabbled around in the dirt in the bad light, looking for them, but what was the use? The magic had to be all out of them by now, and surely they couldn't get Jack or his mother in any sort of trouble.

So he said his transporting spell and went home.

To Rescue a Princess

The wizard was sitting in the storeroom of his tower home, trying to figure out where he could put all the broccoli he'd grown in his garden during the summer. In fact, it had suddenly occurred to him that he didn't even like broccoli very much, and he was wondering why he had planted any at all—other than because it was easy to grow—when he happened to glance out the window.

Someone was coming.

The wizard watched the stranger pick his way

up the steep mountain path. A prince, he decided, because the young man rode a horse, and peasants generally walked. As soon as the youth got closer, the wizard could make out his rich clothes, satin and silk. *Yes,* he thought, *a prince.* Closer still, and he could see the face with its look of haughty self-assurance. *Yes,* he thought, *most certainly a prince.*

The wizard hated unexpected visits, and he hated unexpected visits from royalty most of all. He ducked below the windowsill, just barely peeking over the edge, determined to pretend he wasn't home.

Below him, the prince took out his sword and checked his reflection in the bright blade. Then he used its hilt to rap on the door.

The wizard winced for the just-painted woodwork.

"Yo!" the prince called out. "Open up! I'm here on urgent business."

"They always are," the wizard sighed to himself as the prince knocked more paint off the door with the hilt of his sword. The wizard seri-

ously considered dumping something—prefer-
ably something cold, wet, and extremely slimy—
onto the prince's head.

From behind the wizard a voice hissed,
"Pssst! Stupid! Get your head down before he
sees you." It was his magic mirror, an ancient
thing for which he had paid a year's service to a
bad-tempered duke who had insisted it had an il-
lustrious history, which the duke had never re-
vealed, and great power, also unspecified. So far,
the wizard had found the mirror generally un-
helpful and always insulting, and the only thing it
seemed good for was to periodically announce—
without being asked—that some lady or other
was the fairest in the land.

Even now, the mirror's warning was more
trouble than benefit, for the prince heard it and
looked up, directly at the wizard. "You. Boy.
Open this door, then go fetch your master. I am
the Prince of Talahandra, and I'm in a hurry."

The wizard considered ignoring him, but his
door was at risk. And if he changed the prince
into a toad, somebody was sure to come looking

for him: more unwelcome interruptions. "Thanks a lot," he muttered to the mirror.

He walked down the stairs and unbarred the door.

The Prince of Talahandra swept past him and surveyed the entrance hall with obvious disdain. He glanced at his reflection in an ornamental suit of armor that the wizard kept as a coatrack and patted his already perfect hair. "Well," he said, "where's this wizard of yours?"

The wizard gave a smile that was not especially meant to look friendly. "I'm the wizard."

The prince's nostrils quivered in distaste. "I see." He pursed his lips. "I have a task that needs doing."

"Things to do," the wizard said, "places to go, people to see."

The prince eyed him suspiciously, no doubt suspecting—and rightly so—that the wizard didn't take him seriously. Still, he said, "Yes. Well. This would fit in under 'places to go, things to do,' I suppose. There's a princess who needs rescuing."

The wizard thought that he should have known. But he didn't say so. He said: "From?"

"A dragon."

The wizard tried not to think how terrified the poor girl had to be. He asked, "Do you know the name?"

"Princess Gilbertina of Mustigia."

The wizard sighed. "I meant of the dragon."

"Oh." The prince shrugged. "Do dragons have names?"

The wizard didn't bother to answer. "Do you know if it's a magic dragon?"

Again the prince shrugged. "It breathes fire."

"All dragons breathe fire."

"Oh. Well, I don't see what difference it makes."

"It makes a big difference to whoever's going to rescue the princess."

"I see," said the prince in a tone that hinted he *might,* but if he did, he didn't care. "She's very beautiful, you know."

"The dragon?"

"The princess. I'm told she's the most beautiful woman in the land."

From upstairs, the mirror's voice called out, "Second most beautiful. *The* most beautiful is the milkmaid Aspasia on Farmer Seymour's homestead."

The prince craned his neck to look up the staircase. "Beg your pardon?" he said.

"Never mind that," the wizard interrupted. "What do you mean, *you're told* she's the most beautiful? Don't you know her?"

The prince shook his head.

"Then what, exactly, is your involvement?"

"Her father has promised her hand in marriage and half his kingdom to whoever rescues her."

"But you're asking *me* to rescue her," the wizard pointed out.

"Well. Yes."

"As a special favor to you, on account of our long-standing friendship?"

The prince pouted. "You see, I *did* try. But this dragon lives on a mountain peak that can't be reached except by flying."

"Let me see if I've got this straight. You want me to risk *my* life and limb for *you,* a total stranger, to rescue a princess, whom I also do not know, so that *you* can marry her and win half her father's kingdom."

"Yes, that's it."

"And I'd be doing this for what? Personal glory?"

"Well, no, actually, it wouldn't do for us to publicize that you did the work for me. Then there wouldn't be any sense in *my* marrying the princess and inheriting the kingdom, would there?"

The wizard closed his eyes. "Exactly. So why should I help you?"

"For the personal satisfaction of saving the princess's life?"

Why did they always end up saying something like that? The wizard couldn't get rid of the mental picture of a fierce dragon menacing a poor, frightened princess. "What's the name?"

The prince looked at him uneasily. "Dragon, I don't know. Princess, Gilbertina," he reminded.

The wizard sighed. "The mountain peak."

"Oh, the mountain peak. No, I don't know the name of that, either. I can take you there, though."

The wizard had been hoping to transport himself by magical means rather than travel a bumpy road on the bony back of Farmer Seymour's horse. He sighed again, wishing—as he often did—that his magic wasn't so limited. "Then we'd best get started immediately," he said.

But before he could make a move, the magic mirror shouted out, "Hey, Wizard! I hope you made out a will. I don't want to spend the next five years in a dusty attic while the lawyers sort out your estate."

"Nasty fellow you've got up there," the prince whispered to the wizard. "He doesn't make very much sense, does he? Most beautiful women and all." He looked at the hill that stood between the wizard's property and the village of Saint Wayne the Stutterer. "We wouldn't happen to be near this Farmer Seymour's farm, would we?" he asked.

"That's where we're going for me to borrow a

horse," the wizard said, since the prince hadn't been smart enough to bring two. "Why?"

The prince sucked in his stomach and patted his still perfect hair. "No special reason," he said. "Just wondering."

It took the rest of that day and most of the next for them to reach the mountain where the dragon had taken the princess. The prince, leaning against his horse, was watching the wizard and looking bored.

The wizard held a blue cloud in his left hand. He ran his right over the surface of the cloud, stretching it. But it didn't thin out; it became thicker even as it grew longer. The wizard moved his hand in the other direction, making the cloud taller.

The prince stopped in midyawn to pay closer attention.

The wizard pulled the cloud longer yet: left hand pushing upward, right hand off to the side. The cloud was as big as a whale—and the wizard kept working at it.

"Ahm...," the prince said, and shifted his weight nervously.

The wizard added curves, angles, a leg here, a spiked tail there.

"A dragon," the prince finally said. "You're forming another dragon. Well, that makes sense. Why fight one when you can be fighting two?"

"Shhh," the wizard said, adding extra detail to the scales.

Maybe nobody had ever shushed the prince before. He ignored the wizard's request to be quiet and asked, "What's it going to do, fight the first one?"

"It's only a cloud, an illusion."

"Sounds like it'll be a lot of help."

The wizard glanced up, thinking that maybe it wasn't too late to turn the prince into a toad. Instead, he explained, "Dragons are very territorial. I'll set this one up over there, to the west, and the one that has your princess will go over to investigate. Meanwhile, I'll transform myself into an eagle, fly to the top of the mountain, find the princess, then flash all of us back to the tower."

"The horses, too," the prince reminded him. "Horses are expensive, you know. Don't forget them."

The wizard thought, *If I forget any of us, it won't be the horses.* But he didn't say this; he only floated the dragon up to the distant mountain range where he wanted it.

From above them came an enraged screech.

Wizard and prince ducked as a large green dragon shot out of seemingly nowhere and took off in pursuit of the artificial dragon.

The wizard stretched his arms, whispered a magic word, and felt feathers sprout. He leaped off the edge of the cliff, caught an updraft, and was halfway up the mountainside before he had to start beating his wings.

The cave, which had been invisible from below, was easy to spot, and the wizard landed on the ledge that the dragon must use. He transformed back into a man before entering the cave—so as not to startle the princess, knowing princesses frequently were of a delicate constitution—and he walked inside.

The princess was lying on a pile of pillows embroidered with gold thread and stuffed with gosling feathers. She had a big box of candies by her elbow and was just about to pop one into her mouth when she spotted the wizard. "Hello," she said, her hand stopped in midair. "What's this?"

"I've come to rescue you."

The princess pouted. "Father sent you, didn't he?"

"No," the wizard explained, "actually it was the Prince of Talahandra."

The princess tossed the candy into the air and caught it in her mouth. "Never heard of him."

The wizard watched her chew. And chew. And chew. Then he watched her select another candy and pop *that* into her mouth. Usually rescues did not go like this. Finally he said, "Well?"

"Well, what?"

"Are you coming?"

The princess asked, "Do you mean: Do I consent to be rescued?"

"Yes."

"No."

"No?"

"Yes."

The wizard shook his head to sort this out. "What do you mean, *no*?"

The princess picked up a golden plate and checked her reflection to make sure there was nothing caught between her teeth. She smiled at herself and patted her lovely blond hair. "I mean," she said, as though finally remembering him, "I'm perfectly happy here. The dragon is good to me. It fetches all the sweets I want and takes me for rides on its back, flying all over the countryside, and I've got even nicer things here than I do at home, where I have to share with my two ugly sisters." She gestured to the pile of dragon treasure upon which her pillows rested. "I imagine my father's promised to let my rescuer marry me, hasn't he? He's old-fashioned that way. Well, I do not choose to be rescued in the name of some fat old prince who's too lazy to come and rescue me himself." She studied the box of candies and selected another morsel. "Sorry," she mumbled, her mouth full.

The wizard tapped his foot impatiently, knowing that if he just flashed on back home, the prince would eventually follow him there and never give him any rest. "Look," he said wearily, "the Prince of Talahandra is not fat or old. He's really very handsome, and quite rich."

The princess looked interested, but still skeptical.

The wizard added, "The prince is also very intelligent and resourceful, and he hired me rather than coming himself so that there would be less danger to you."

"I don't know," the princess said. "I *do* enjoy the flying."

"Besides," the wizard said smoothly, though he was making it up as he went along, "some of the most famous candy makers in the world are in the kingdom of Talahandra. Please," he urged. "The dragon will be back any moment."

Slowly, reluctantly, the princess stood up, putting the box of candy under her arm. "Do you think I'll like this prince?" she asked.

This time, the wizard could answer in all truthfulness. "Believe me, you were made for each other." Then, as she started stuffing diamond-encrusted combs and other trinkets into her pockets, the wizard added, "And I have a fine mirror that will make a perfect engagement present for the two of you."

"Oh, thank you," she said, munching on a caramel.

A week later, the wizard was lying half asleep on a hammock in the backyard of his tower home. The summer was almost half over. A few more weeks and his students would be back for the fall semester. He smiled, thinking that he had missed them, though he would never tell them so.

Something large and heavy dropped onto his chest.

"Hello, old friend," came the familiar and unwelcome voice of his magic mirror. "Getting lazy in your old age, I see."

The wizard opened his eyes and saw Princess Gilbertina standing there, tapping her foot, her arms folded defiantly before her.

"It didn't work out," she said. "The engagement is off, and I want you to take this piece of garbage off my hands."

The wizard had had all the breath knocked out of him, so he couldn't point out that the garbage in question was, in fact, already out of her hands and sitting on his chest.

He eased the heavy mirror to the side, off the edge of the hammock.

"Easy, big fellow," the mirror grumbled.

The wizard found he could breathe again. "What seems to be the problem?" he asked.

"This stupid mirror of yours is a troublemaker."

"*No!*" gasped the wizard, trying to sound surprised.

"It put all sorts of crazy ideas into the head of the Prince of Talahandra. He was supposed to marry me, but all he does is hang around Farmer Seymour's barn, sighing and writing bad poetry over that milkmaid—who is *not*, I might add, all that great."

"I see," said the wizard.

"After all"—the princess fluffed her hair—"even this stupid mirror acknowledges that I'm the second most beautiful woman in the land, and the Prince of Talahandra is only the eighth most handsome man. The mirror told me so."

"I'm sorry things didn't work out for you and the prince," the wizard said. "But I don't see why you're here."

"I want to go home to my dragon."

"Oh." The wizard looked at her pouting but determined face. "Ahm—"

"And you're going to take me there."

He started to open his mouth to protest, but she began speaking louder and faster and pointed her finger at him. "This is all your fault. *You're* the one who talked me into leaving, and *you're* the one who gave me this miserable mirror." She lifted her chin and spoke in a most regal tone. "I am ready for you to take me home *now.*"

It was, the wizard knew, the only way he'd

ever get rid of her. He said the magic word that transported both of them to the dragon's cave. However, he put too much energy into his spell, and not only were he and the princess transported, but also the hammock, the mirror, two nearby rosebushes, and his clothesline, on which he'd been airing out his winter underwear.

One thing he did not bring was the pair of trees to which the hammock had been attached. The hammock dropped to the floor of the cave, carrying the wizard with it.

"Thank you," said Princess Gilbertina.

The green dragon, who had been sitting with his back to the cave entrance, whirled around at the sound of her voice and shrieked in surprise and dismay.

"Yes," the princess said, "I'm back."

The dragon closed his eyes, covered them with his claws, and backed away. "I'm not going to look at you!" he said. "You're not going to fool me again."

The wizard picked himself up from the tangle

of his hammock. He looked from the dragon to the princess. "I have the feeling I've missed something here."

"Do you see what she's trying to do?" the dragon demanded, peeking out at the wizard from between clawed fingers. "I knew it was a mistake, but her golden hair was too much for me to resist, and she knows it." He shrugged self-consciously. "Dragons are pushovers for gold, you know."

"Come, come," the princess said to the dragon. "Won't you give me one little smile?" She scratched him behind the ears.

The dragon shook his head. " 'Rescue me,' you said. 'Save me from dying of boredom,' you said. 'Take me flying, and you'll be my lifelong friend.' Ha! More like your servant. Well, I got tired of waiting on you, and telling you over and over how beautiful you are, and my back and wings got sore from carrying you around all day. Then I saw that wizard and that prince, and I knew what was going on, and it seemed like the perfect opportunity. I chased their fake dragon on purpose so they'd get you out of here."

The princess pouted. "That's not very nice." She smiled. "But I forgive you." She tickled him under his chin. "Do you forgive me?"

The huge dragon squirmed. "Yes. Now just get out of here."

"Come on," she wheedled, "give me one little smile. One cute little dragon smile. Wizard, don't you think this is the cutest dragon you've ever seen?"

The wizard didn't know how to answer, but luckily the mirror did. The mirror said, "Actually, he is. He's the number one, fairest-looking dragon in the land."

The dragon's eyes popped open. "Really?"

"I am never incorrect. And I certainly never lie."

"What a charming mirror!" the dragon cried. "Isn't that a charming mirror? And gold, too. Whose is it?"

"Mine," the princess purred.

The dragon turned his large green eyes to her.

She tipped her head demurely, so that all the dragon could see was her golden hair.

The dragon smiled.

The wizard picked up his hammock and whispered his magic word.

Back in his own yard, he refastened the hammock ropes to the trees. Hopefully the princess would try to be easier to get along with, and the dragon would try to be more patient, and she and he and the mirror would be happy together.

The wizard lay down with his face to the late-afternoon sun. And with luck the Prince of Talahandra wouldn't come looking for her but would marry the milkmaid on Farmer Seymour's farm.

The wizard hummed to himself. If that happened, he had just the wedding present for them, something he had picked up on one of his journeys but for which he had never found a use: a single glass slipper....

Wizard and Ghost

The wizard was in his garden, tying pieces of string around fragments of junk metal and then nailing the flapping contraptions onto wooden stakes. Mostly he used bits of rusted armor that he'd once accepted in trade from a down-on-his-luck knight too poor to pay for a good-fortune spell; but there were also a few burnt and badly dented pots, because cooking was not one of the wizard's strong points. He was hoping that the noise made by these scraps of metal rattling in the wind would be enough to frighten away the rabbits, who were particularly bold this year. They'd jumped over the little fence he'd built in May, and they'd gnawed the feet off the scarecrow he'd set up in June, and they'd made nests out of the snippets of his hair he'd scattered about in July. Here it was August, and though his principles inclined him against using magic to harm living creatures, there weren't many vegetables left, and he *was* getting tempted.

He looked up from his hammering when a man came tromping through the vegetables. The stranger seemed not to notice at all that he was in a garden, so that he stepped on carrots, which might conceivably survive the trampling, and tomato plants, which probably would not.

The wizard would have shouted to the man to watch where he put his feet, but he couldn't. His mother had always warned him that holding nails clenched between his teeth was dangerous, though most likely her chief worry had been that he would accidentally swallow one.

"Halt!" the wizard tried to call out from around the nails.

The stranger must have taken the garbled word as greeting, for he responded, "Hello right back to you!" and kept on walking toward him.

The wizard spat the nails out into his hand, but by then the man was standing before him, asking, "Are you the wizard or the gardener?"

"I *used* to be a gardener," the wizard snapped. "But it looks as though that isn't going to work out."

Apparently sarcasm was beyond his visitor. "So you're not the wizard? I was told the wizard lived here. Do you know where the wizard *does* live?"

"I *am* the wizard."

The man looked annoyed. "Well, then, why didn't you say so? Do you like going around trying to confuse people?"

The wizard refrained from pointing out that some people are easier to confuse than others. He sighed and simply said, "Just watch your feet, and tell me why you're here."

The man looked down at his feet. If he noticed that he was ankle deep in a baby lettuce, he didn't say so. He said, "My master, Duke Snell, has sent me to fetch you to his castle in Northrup."

"I don't know Duke Snell," the wizard said, though he knew where Northrup was, in the furthermost reach of the realm. He already wasn't impressed—neither with the manner of the invitation, nor with the messenger, who was still looking at his feet, evidently taking the wizard's comment to watch his feet as a continuing order. Either Duke Snell employed people who were not strong on thinking ability, or he gave capricious orders that he expected to be followed exactly. Neither instance spoke well of the man.

The duke's messenger assured the wizard, "But the duke knows you. Or of you, at any rate. There's a problem at the castle, and he needs you to fix it."

"Really?" The wizard was beginning to lose patience. "And what makes him think I will?"

Still staring at his feet, perhaps concerned that a spell was about to affect them and apparently unaware of the wizard's growing indignation, the messenger explained, "The king is coming for a visit next week, and Duke Snell wants to make sure the castle is safe."

This wasn't exactly an answer to the wizard's question, but the wizard *did* know the king, who was not the kind of man to give frivolous orders or surround himself with people who didn't know how to think. The wizard didn't want anything bad to happen to him. So he asked, "What kind of problem does Duke Snell have?"

"The castle is being haunted."

The wizard hadn't had much experience with hauntings, for there are many more *reports* of ghosts than actual ghosts. In fact, he suspected there was probably some more ordinary explanation for whatever the duke thought was happening. Still, he found his curiosity prickled, and he asked, "Who's the castle being haunted by?"

"A ghost."

The wizard sighed. "Who has died recently?"

"That's just the problem," the man said. "Or one of them: Nobody has. Well, I mean, I suppose *some*body *some*where in the whole wide world has died in recent weeks, but none of the people from the castle. Will you come?"

The wizard sighed again. It probably wasn't a real ghost—ghosts are actually quite rare. And there were things he needed to do around here before his students returned from their summer holiday, but he was intrigued. That, and he wanted to keep the king safe. "All right," he said.

"Good," the man told him. "Can I stop watching my feet now?"

The wizard resisted the temptation to see how long this could last and said, "Yes."

Though the wizard had been to the region of Northrup, he hadn't ever been to Duke Snell's castle, so he couldn't transport himself directly there. He had the duke's messenger name off nearby landmarks and recognized Standish Wood as a place he *had* visited. So he saved himself three days of traveling on Farmer Seymour's ill-natured horse by using his transportation spell to get to the town of Frisbane, which sat between where Standish Wood ended and the great northern plains started. He also saved himself the company of the duke's man, claiming—though it wasn't true—that his spell only worked on himself.

In Frisbane he cast the spell to make himself look more wizardly, then he hired a boat. This took half a day to get him east a fraction of the distance he had traveled instantly by spell. It was late afternoon before the boatman announced, "The duke's castle."

The castle sat on an island in the river. The wizard saw the way was blocked by two water gates, one before and one beyond the castle, and there was a guard at each gate, and a mechanism to raise and lower the gates.

The nearer guard approached and motioned them to come in toward the shore. He was bearing a tally sheet and a bored expression. As though he'd proclaimed this a thousand times a day, the guard called to them: "One-silver-penny toll for traveling through the moat area." A silver penny was enough to buy a good sanding and painting for this boat, which it could probably use, and some nice soft seat cushions—which it definitely needed.

"I'm not traveling *through* the moat area," the boatman said. "I simply need to row up to the castle mooring area to drop off this gentleman here."

The guard made a check mark on his tally sheet. "Two-silver-penny toll for lingering in the moat area," he said.

The wizard leaned forward and explained, "Duke Snell asked me to come."

The guard waited a few seconds before saying, "And your point is?..."

Surely this shouldn't be so complicated, the wizard thought. "The point is: If I'm the duke's guest, we shouldn't have to pay a toll."

"Yeah," the guard agreed in a mocking tone. "And dogs shouldn't get fleas, apples shouldn't have worms, and new shoes shouldn't pinch."

The wizard considered transforming himself into a bird that could fly over the water to the castle, but he didn't want to cause a scene because he didn't know if the duke wanted people knowing he had hired a wizard. Sometimes, when one works for royalty, one needs to be discreet. Besides, there was probably a three-silver-penny toll for using airspace.

The boatman was obviously waiting for the wizard to pay the toll, for which the wizard couldn't blame him; otherwise the man would lose half the fare he'd just earned.

The wizard took two coins from what the duke's messenger had paid for him to come, and handed them over to the guard.

The guard checked off something else on his sheet, then turned the cogwheel that raised the gate.

The gate rose, creaking and dripping.

Once they were through, the guard drew yet another mark on his sheet. "Proceed directly to the mooring area," he warned sternly. "There's a fine for loitering."

"Why is that not a surprise?" the boatman muttered as he pulled on the oars.

"Careful," the wizard whispered. "There's probably a sarcasm tax."

The boatman grunted but said no more as he rowed the few short strokes to the mooring.

The wizard climbed out of the boat—without getting any assistance from the castle guard who stood about three feet away and looked as though his entire job was to pretend to be a statue.

I'm not having a good feeling about this whole business, the wizard told himself. *I should probably just turn around and go home right now*—which would be considerably easier than getting here, because he could use his transporting spell. But he was still curious about the haunting, and he *had* been paid already. *I'll give it a little longer,* he told himself.

"State your business," said the castle guard who was impersonating a statue.

Since Snell's messenger had never referred to him by name, the wizard suspected Snell didn't know what his name was, so he simply said, "I am the wizard"—calculating there was no use being so discreet that the guard wouldn't let him in.

This guard had a list, too, and one of the entries must have read "The Wizard," for he made a check mark and said, "You may proceed inside. Someone will show you to Duke Snell's audience hall. Tips, by the way, are gratefully accepted."

"That's good to know," the wizard said.

As the wizard started up the stairs to the castle, he heard the water gate guard tell the boatman, "One-silver-penny toll for leaving the moat area." The wizard shook his head and entered the castle, suspecting that he and Snell were very unlikely to hit it off.

The wizard waited and waited and waited in the audience hall until he very seriously considered transporting himself out of there, ghost or not. He suspected he wouldn't get in to see the duke unless he bribed one of the guards, and he was determined not to do that. On his way home he could always drop in on the king, he thought, with the warning that Snell's castle might not be safe. He was distracted by wondering whether the gate guards would charge the king for passage, and while he was thinking about that, Snell finally sent for him.

The duke was a tall, good-looking man, with a quick smile. His sandy-colored hair tended to fall forward so that he had to repeatedly toss his head back to fling the hair out of his eyes. The wizard supposed that young women might find this charming. He found himself immediately annoyed with the man.

"Ah, Wizard!" Snell said. "Thank you for coming so quickly. I trust you found the trip easy."

The wizard smiled back at him. "Well, yes, until your castle guards started extorting money from me."

Snell gave a concerned frown. "The tolls?" he asked. "A necessary evil, I'm afraid. I have just inherited this duchy and need to raise money to support public works, such as schools and road improvement, which were sadly neglected by my predecessor."

The last time the wizard had visited the region of Northrup, he had not noticed anything wrong with the roads. And judging by what he saw of fine tapestries and gold and silver ornaments about the castle, the wizard suspected that the duke's philosophy might well be that improvement starts at home.

The duke was saying, "But *you* should not have been charged since I invited you. You must demand your fee back from the guards."

I? the wizard thought, suspecting how far that would get him—suspecting *Snell* knew how far that would get him. But he didn't say that; he asked, "So you are just recently made duke?"

Snell nodded.

"And now you are troubled by a ghost."

Again Snell nodded. "Despite the fact," the duke added, "that no one from the castle has died recently."

Though he suspected there was a more ordinary explanation than haunting for whatever was troubling the castle, the wizard asked, "Could the spirit be that of the previous duke?"

"It could," Snell agreed, "but I seriously doubt it because the man is not dead." Snell smiled at the wizard, and the wizard smiled back to indicate he found this clever, though in reality he thought the duke pompous and full of himself. "I did not inherit this castle," Snell clarified, "but was given it by Duke Lawrence as a reward for good service. He has other lands."

"How lucky for everyone." The wizard made a point of not asking what good deed or bravery the duke had done, which, he guessed, the duke expected him to be dying to hear about. "So who do you suspect the ghost is, and what might be its business?"

"No idea," Snell said. "That's why I hired you."

"What does this ghost do?"

"Oh, it moans a lot, and drips water in the passageways."

"Moans," the wizard repeated. "Water." The duke wasn't being very helpful. "Old houses make noises. And are you sure you don't simply have a leak?"

"Fairly sure," the duke said. "Come take a look at my former quarters."

He led the wizard into another room, a bedroom. The bed curtains had been yanked off their rings, the wall hangings had been slashed to shreds, and all the items that had previously sat on top of the chests and dressers had been hurled to the floor.

"Someone doesn't like you," the wizard observed. Of course, *he* didn't like the duke, either, but this looked like a situation that might be dangerous. "No idea who?" the wizard prompted.

"No idea," the duke echoed. "That's the second time you've asked. Do you want to hear the rest of it?"

"Oh, why not?" the wizard said, irritated at the way the duke seemed in love with his own voice. "Now that I've traveled all this way."

Snell didn't note or at least didn't comment on the wizard's surliness. "The rest of it," he said, "is that the window was barred and the door locked when this happened."

"Someone with a key, then," the wizard speculated, still looking for a reasonable explanation.

"And a tendency to be invisible," Snell said. "I was in the room at the time."

That got the wizard's attention. "Maybe you'd better start at the beginning."

With the look of a man who is vastly impressed with himself, Duke Snell said, "After I rescued Duke Lawrence's daughter Cordelia from a band of bandits in Standish Wood, the duke rewarded me with this land and gave me his daughter in marriage."

The wizard was not surprised that the duke had found a way to bring the conversation back to his own accomplishments.

"Soon after we were wed and moved into this castle, we began to hear moaning noises, at first very faint. But every night the sounds grew louder and they started earlier and lasted longer. Then we began finding water in the castle hallways and some of the rooms, at first just a small puddle here and there. But those grew, too, till there were huge wet tracks—most often, I must say, directly outside my bedroom door."

There were several questions that plagued the wizard. The one he settled on was, "Tracks? As in a man's footprints? Or a woman's? Could you tell if they were made by boots, or shoes, or bare feet?"

The duke was shaking his head. "Not footprints. More like a trail of water. As though the ghost is dragging something behind him, like a wide, sopping-wet blanket."

"Why would the ghost be dragging a blanket?" the wizard asked.

"I didn't say he *is*," the duke complained. "You're not listening properly. How can you solve this problem if you repeat questions and don't listen properly? I didn't say the ghost is dragging a wet blanket behind him—I said he's leaving a track *like* a dragged wet blanket. You need to improve your listening skills." Then he added, "Sometimes the walls are wet, too."

To prove he was listening, the wizard asked, "As though the ghost is slinging the wet blanket against the walls?"

"I don't think you're taking this very seriously," Snell said, a hint of whine coming into his voice. "What am I paying you all this money for if you're not going to take me seriously?"

The wizard was tempted to answer that you can't pay someone to take you seriously, and that—besides—the duke wasn't paying him all that much. Instead, he said, "Moans and then water. Go on."

Snell said, "Then things started breaking. *My* things. I mean, everything in the castle is *mine*— Duke Lawrence declared it so. But my personal things. Then that got worse and worse, too, until I sent for you. You see where it ended last night"— the duke waved his arm dramatically about the ruined room—"while I was waiting for you."

The wizard didn't say, "Don't blame me for living three days away." He said, "You said you saw this happen."

"I'd put wax in my ears to block the noise of the moaning," Snell explained, "or I'd never have been able to sleep. But I woke up when that huge stained-glass panel came crashing down onto the floor. Stained glass is expensive, you know."

"I can imagine." Snell was the type, the wizard thought, who wasn't satisfied with surrounding himself with expensive things—he wanted everyone to know he was surrounded by expensive things.

"I sat up in bed—and before you ask, no, I definitely wasn't dreaming. I was fully awake."

The wizard smiled innocently.

"And then I saw those things lift up from my nightstand, one by one, with no hand touching them. And then the nightstand tipped over. And then it burst apart, as though someone had smashed it with a gigantic hammer."

"A ghost hammer...," the wizard speculated doubtfully.

Snell sighed impatiently. "Or maybe the ghost just jumped on it with both feet."

"More likely," the wizard agreed. "Did your wife see all this, too?"

"Duchess Cordelia has returned to her parents' home for safety's sake," the duke said. "But this is not my imagination, if that's what you're hinting at."

"The thought never crossed my mind," the wizard lied. "Have you thought of returning to *your* parents' home?"

Duke Snell sniffed as though speaking of his parents reminded him of a bad odor. "My parents are woodcutters—simple people who live in a simple house."

The wizard guessed that meant no, Snell had *not* considered moving back in with them. He noticed that Snell said nothing about his in-laws inviting him to stay with them. "Still," he said, "if you left, then we could learn if the ghost would stay here or follow you."

"Why would it follow me?" Snell asked.

"Why would it ruin your things?" the wizard countered.

The duke made that bad-smell face again.

The wizard continued, "Either the ghost is haunting this castle, or it's haunting you. Ghosts usually remain near where they died, yet you said none of the castle inhabitants has died recently."

"Right so far," the duke said, sounding impatient. "As...I...said...already."

"But sometimes ghosts haunt the person responsible for their death."

"I haven't killed anyone," Snell protested.

The wizard wanted to ask, "Are you sure you haven't bored anyone to death?" but instead asked, "What about the bandits you rescued your wife from?"

Snell shook his head. "I didn't kill any of them. They ran off into the woods."

"Lucky Cordelia," the wizard said. "Lucky you. Lucky bandits."

"And I didn't know any of them," Snell added, though it had never occurred to the wizard to ask. "They wore masks when they captured Cordelia, and they kept her blindfolded in their camp so she couldn't identify any of them."

"And you happened upon their woodland camp," the wizard said, "woodcutter's son that you are. But you never saw their faces, either."

"That is correct," Snell said.

The wizard suspected that a man of Snell's ambition would never have been satisfied with the life of a woodcutter. He might, in fact, have been one of the bandits himself, and might have convinced or paid his companions to run away so

★ Vivian Vande Velde ★

that he could appear as a hero to the rescued young woman and her family. But the wizard had no proof of this, and—besides—that didn't explain the ghost.

"If you won't go to your parents or to your wife's parents," the wizard said, "is there somewhere else you can spend the night?"

"This is most irksome," the duke complained. He paused, looking at the room in ruins about him. "I suppose I could make arrangements to stay at my hunting lodge."

Despite his casual words, he was on the road within the hour.

The wizard had lost the greater part of the day traveling, and it was already time for supper. He ate with the castle inhabitants in the Great Hall (for a silver penny) and spoke to the servants, whose stories matched Duke Snell's: They, too, had heard moans that grew louder with each passing night, and had found the hallways slick with wet.

94

"Which hallways?" he asked the servants as they cleaned up after the meal.

Mostly the ones between the entryway and Duke Snell's private rooms, they all agreed.

"Interesting," the wizard said. "What kind of moans?"

The servants looked from him to one another. One tried to imitate the sound—a loud, mournful warble at which some of the others nodded or said, "Yes," or, "More or less," or, "Not exactly."

"Inhuman moans," another of them finally said, and that was something to which all nodded in agreement.

"Moans to make the hair on your head stand up and walk right off," added the servant who was sweeping the floor. He was bald, which might have meant he should be taken seriously. Or not.

The wizard asked, "Who was the last person to die here?"

The servants laid down dishes, platters, washrags, and brooms, put their heads together, and tried to work this out. The mother of one of the baker's assistants, they finally came up with: an elderly woman who had died in her sleep during the week between Christmas and New Year's—months before Snell ever made his timely appearance in the bandits' camp.

An unlikely candidate, the wizard thought. Usually people who died of old age did not become night-roaming ghosts. Ghosts were most often the victims of sudden, violent death. And why would a spirit have lingered on earth almost eight months before making its presence known, and then take out its frustrations on Snell's possessions?

And what about the water?

"Do you know of any recent drownings?" the wizard asked.

The servants were getting fidgety and restless because he was keeping them from their work, and a few went back to the kitchen while he was busy with the others. No, the remaining servants told him. Maybe at one of the little towns that bordered the river, but no one from the castle.

They didn't travel up and down the river much, letting people come to them, instead. And no one swam in the area because of the moat monster.

The wizard hadn't realized there was a moat monster, or he'd have been nervous on the boat that afternoon. "Could the monster have eaten someone?" the wizard asked.

The servants' looks indicated they found this unlikely.

"No one's missing," one pointed out.

"You don't see too much of the creature," another said. "*I* haven't seen him in weeks."

"He's shy," yet another put in. The rest of the servants nodded.

"We rarely see him."

"Just, once in a while, the top of his head as he peeks out of the water, or the hump of his back or tail."

"He's a faithful, gentle beast, and wouldn't eat anyone."

The wizard, who'd had encounters with dogs whose owners insisted they were friendly, kept his doubts to himself.

The evening got darker and quieter, and the wizard went to the bedroom the duke had vacated to spend the night there, to avoid the silver-penny lodging fee and to see if the ghost would turn up even with the duke away.

Either that, the wizard thought, or the ghost had followed Snell to the hunting lodge, which would prove something, though the wizard was not sure exactly what. If that had happened, the duke was certain to be mightily annoyed—which was a thought that cheered the wizard considerably as he settled down in the duke's large comfortable chair to wait.

The wizard had fallen asleep when he was awakened by a low, sad moaning—something close to, but not exactly like, what the servant had demonstrated for him. The sound seemed to come from outside, but when the wizard unshuttered the window, all he saw was the moon reflected in the water of the still moat, and the surrounding woods on the far shore.

But even as the wizard saw there was nothing to see, the moaning moved—so that now it came from beneath the castle, echoing hollowly off the cold stones.

The wizard stayed where he was, and sure enough the sound came toward him: working its way from the first-floor entry, through the Great Hall, up the stairs, coming closer and closer, down the far hallway till it came around the corner and down the final hall to the duke's personal rooms.

The wizard could hear the moaning, loud enough to vibrate his bones, just on the other side of the bedroom door.

He considered opening the door, but according to the duke, that shouldn't be necessary.

In another moment a damp spot appeared on the door, and on the floor in front of it—a big spot. A huge spot. A spot too massive to be made by a ghost that was the size of any man. Some unseen thing—something the size of a small house—was standing there, dripping: The wizard could see the drops of water once they were shed, starting from a height disconcertingly close to the fifteen-foot-high ceiling.

The moaning, which had been coming from high above the wizard's head, paused...

...then resumed, slightly softer, as though the ghost had turned its back on the wizard, as though it was heading back through the door.

Of course it's leaving, the wizard thought. *It was looking for Snell.*

"Wait!" the wizard called.

The moaning stopped entirely, but the dripping water did not.

"I'm here to help you," the wizard said. *Help get rid of you* was what he meant, but the way to get rid of a ghost is to settle whatever is bothering it.

Judging by the dripping water, the unseen creature, whatever it was, remained where it was.

"Can you speak?" the wizard asked.

The moaning resumed.

The wizard, realizing the moaning was the creature's speech, cast a spell so that he could understand the speech of animals. "There. Now can you tell me who you are?"

"I am Guardian," the deep but quiet voice said. "It is my duty to protect this den."

"Den?" the wizard echoed. Had the castle been built on top of a dragon's lair? But usually dragons preferred caves in high places. And the castle was not new enough to have recently disturbed a dragon's nest.

The ghostly voice repeated, "This den. And all those of your kind who dwell within."

It meant the castle. It was calling the castle the closest word it had to "home" or "dwelling."

The moat monster, the wizard realized. It hadn't killed anyone—*it* was the one who had died. Everyone had been trying to think of *people* who had died. And all the while this poor dead thing was unable to stop its attempts to continue the task that had been set for it.

The wizard said, "It is good that you take your duty so seriously, but now it is time for you to rest."

"I cannot," the ghost of the moat monster said.

"Did another wizard bespell you?"

The moat monster said, "There were words spoken in silver light, with the scent of jasmine and the feel of sun-warmed pebbles—the way you spoke just now to allow yourself to understand my speech. Those words said I was to be Guardian, and I was to protect this den and all who dwell within for the rest of my natural life."

The wizard hadn't been aware that magic words had scent or texture. "Well," he said, "it is difficult to be the bearer of bad news, but I have to tell you…" He sighed, never before having had to tell anyone, *You died.*

But he didn't have to say it now, either. Apparently the creature already knew it was dead. "'My natural life,'" it repeated. "My kind normally lives through a thousand revolutions of this earth around the sun: time of rain and new growth, time of heat, time of leaves turning bright colors, and time of snow. But I lived only a hundred cycles."

That was the trouble with spells: Sometimes they just went on and on.

The wizard said, "Others' spells can be very tricky to overcome, but I can try to unravel the spell that ties you here."

Silence.

Not that the wizard was used to thunderous applause at his proclamations, but he had expected the moat monster to say *some*thing. Had it left the room after all? Half suspecting there would be no answer to this, either, the wizard asked, "Don't you want to move on to the next stage of being?"

The moat monster's voice came soft as a sigh, but still from the same spot. It said, "A hundred cycles out of a thousand is not very long at all."

"I realize that," the wizard said. Then he thought to ask, "What did you die of?"

"Bad meat," the monster said.

The wizard decided it might be rude to mention that this was a risk taken by those who ate their meat raw. But then he remembered how the servants had insisted the monster was a gentle creature, and he realized the monster had said "meat," not "fish," and he thought to wonder where a moat-bound, gentle-natured monster would get its meat. He asked, "Bad as in spoiled?"

"Bad as in poisoned." The monster sighed. "I didn't eat it, of course. My nose and my eyes could tell there was something wrong. But the poison spread from the pieces of meat into the water itself. I avoided the tainted area, but then more pieces were thrown in, here and there, all about the water that surrounds the den, and the fish either swam away or sickened and died. I am not permitted to swim away."

"Duke Snell," the wizard surmised. "He wanted to set up the gates in the water so that he could charge tolls and make money to buy himself fine things and make himself impressive in the eyes of others." For a moment he thought he was explaining things to the monster, but then, looking about the room with all its broken things, he realized the monster knew.

"I cannot give you back the life that was taken from you," the wizard said, "but I can make Duke Snell pay for it."

"How?" the monster said.

"Wait and see," the wizard said, for he knew that the monster would not be pleased with his solution.

The next morning, as soon as Duke Snell returned, the wizard told him to order all the inhabitants—servants and hangers-on alike—to leave the castle.

"Why?" Snell demanded.

"I'm going to rid the castle of its ghost," the wizard explained.

"I thought you were supposed to do that last night," Snell complained.

The wizard forced a pleasant smile. "Ghosts are more powerful in the dark. Daytime is the proper time for dispersing them."

Snell sighed. "Well, it will take most of the day to get all my possessions out of the castle."

"Oh, your things can stay," the wizard said. "People can't. I don't want to get too technical here, but organic life-forms might tend to…soak up some of the residual"—the wizard was having to think quickly—"ahm…residue from the magic. But possessions—perfectly safe."

Snell asked skeptically, "Are you sure?"

"Didn't you pay me that great big salary because I'm the expert?"

Snell looked as though he was trying to work out whether he had paid too much or whether the wizard was being sarcastic, but he gave the order. The wizard directed everyone to wait on the far bank of the river, across from the island on which the castle stood.

They were just starting their picnic lunch when the wizard began to weave his spell. It was a variation of his transportation spell, and he worked carefully, a little bit at a time, affecting the back of the castle, where the people couldn't see.

It was, in fact, the moat monster who first realized what he was doing. Bound by spells to protect the castle, the ghost creature rose out of the moat with an angry roar and an explosion of water, so fast that the water clung to its sides, giving shape to its insubstantial form: a huge, rounded body with a long neck, and wide-open jaws that dripped what might have been saliva, or moat water.

People pointed and screamed, and the wizard took the opportunity to transport a whole section from the lower back part of the castle away from there and into his own yard. Eventually, he could use the stones to build a garden wall that those unruly rabbits would need wings to get over, but that wasn't his chief goal. His purpose was to weaken the castle's structure, and that's exactly what happened. A huge crack appeared on the front face of the castle as the entire building began to tip backward over the missing section.

"Wizard!" Snell screamed across the water at him. "Look what's happening!"

The water had run off the moat monster so that it was once more invisible. But something knocked the wizard off his feet, which he figured must be the moat monster butting him with its head. Still, however intent the ghost was on protecting the castle, it was not substantial enough—especially in the daylight—to cause the wizard harm.

There was a resounding *crack!* as the castle, unable to support its own weight, split apart. Stones hurtled outward, which was the real reason the wizard hadn't wanted anyone else standing on the front lawn. And then, in a cloud of dust that started at the ground and built upward, the castle tumbled to the ground.

"You incompetent ninny!" Snell screamed. "My castle! My beautiful castle! Duke Lawrence will never give me another one! Cordelia will never stay married to me if she has to live in a woodcutter's cottage!"

"Sorry," the wizard said. If Snell had been close enough to hear, he might have assumed the wizard was apologizing for not being able to save the castle from the ghost; he was never likely to guess that the wizard was, in fact, apologizing to the ghost.

The wizard picked himself up off the grass and walked to the edge of the island. "Did you see that creature come up out of the water?" he called over to the people on the other side. He knew they had—they'd been screaming. "Who would have thought it could knock the castle down like that? I never heard of anything like that ever happening before. So, under the circumstances, Duke Snell, I'm not going to charge you the second half of my fee."

The wizard didn't wait for Snell's sputtering to form itself into words. "Good-bye, then," he said cheerily, and faced the other way, to speak to the moat monster. "Sorry," the wizard said to it again. "That seemed the best way to free you of your duty to protect the castle, and at the same time to punish Duke Snell."

Of course, he couldn't see if the creature was actually there, and for a few long moments he wondered whether the destruction of the castle had dispersed its spirit, for there was no answer. Then Guardian's quiet voice said, "If I had known what you intended, I would have tried to stop you."

"Which is why I didn't discuss my plan with you," the wizard explained. "The castle is gone;

those who lived there must now go elsewhere. The spell that held you as Guardian has no more power over you."

"Still…" The monster sighed. "It would have been nice to stay in this world for at least a few more of the thousand cycles I should have had."

"Stay, then," the wizard said, "for as long as *you* want to." He glanced over his shoulder and saw that two of the castle guards were rowing a boat toward the island shore. Snell was also in the boat, shaking his fist at him.

The moat monster said, "But there are too many bad memories here. If I knew of another river, or a lake…But it is difficult for my kind to travel over land…"

The wizard had glimpsed its huge body and small legs. He offered, "I could take you to a place I know of: A nice, deep, secluded lake, with clean water, but peat beneath. That way, if people *did* come, you could roll yourself in the peat and let people glimpse you—the way the people here glimpsed you before the water ran down off your sides—and they would be frightened away."

"You can get me there with the silver words that smell of jasmine and feel like sun-warmed pebbles?" When the wizard nodded, the moat monster said, "Then I would like that."

With the sound of Snell's rowboat scraping its bottom in the shallows behind him, the wizard did a double transporting spell to the lake he'd described.

"It's a lovely place to spend a few more cycles before I'm ready to move on," the moat monster said, splashing its head into the water then out again quickly, so that the wizard could momentarily glimpse its smallish head atop its long neck. "And I will remember how to make my body visible if I want to play tricks, once in a while, on those of your kind who may come here. Thank you, Wizard."

"You're welcome, Guardian," the wizard said. He interrupted the spell to transport himself back home only long enough to say, "Enjoy the lake. By the way, it's called Ness."

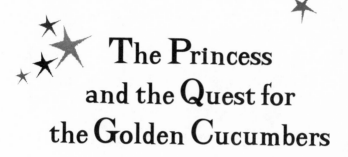

The Princess
and the Quest for
the Golden Cucumbers

When the king and queen of his own land invited the wizard for tea at their castle, he knew he should probably make some sort of excuse. "School will be starting next week," he could say. "So much to do," he could say. After all, he knew they had a daughter and he'd had more than enough problems with princesses this summer.

Still, it wouldn't do to get them angry. So he packed a huge box of broccoli to give the queen as a hostess present and showed up exactly on time.

The princess was late.

Waiting for her, the wizard made the teapot rise up from the table and float to a position directly above the king's cup.

The king and queen had invited him here to ask a favor, he was sure of it, and no doubt the smart thing to do was to downplay his magical abilities, but it was hard to resist the temptation to show off, especially since his wise old wizard disguise wouldn't work with them—they knew his true age. In any case, they were looking beyond him, out the big French windows that opened onto the flower garden. He had barely glimpsed the young woman riding the large horse when the king tapped him on the knee.

"A lovely girl, the princess," the king said. "Lovely, in her own way. But not quite what one could call...ahm, exactly, er..."

"Marriageable," the queen suggested.

The king winced. "Marriageable," he agreed. "The thing is, she has no suitors. That is, none that we've found suitable, that was…ahm, as it were, ah…"

"Willing to ask for her hand," the queen finished.

The king shrugged apologetically. "We're hoping you can do something about it," he said in a hurried whisper as the princess slid off the horse and jumped over a low hedge to enter by the window. She was tall, that was the wizard's first impression, and had long frizzy hair of a rather mousy brown. "Hello," she said before the wizard could notice much else about her. "Sorry I'm late, but Farmer Seymour's cart was stuck—"

"Yes, yes, my dear." The queen looked disapprovingly at her daughter's pants and brushed at her dusty sleeve. "You should have let Farmer Seymour get his cart out from wherever it was stuck by himself. Say hello to the wizard."

The wizard, who was not short, stood up and found himself at eye level with the princess's chin.

"Pleased to meet you," the princess said, and shook his hand before he could kiss hers. "Kind of young for a wizard, aren't you?"

The queen made a *tut* sound. "Theodora, don't be rude." She turned back to the wizard. "I know that Theodora—"

"Teddy," the princess interrupted.

"Theodora," the queen continued, "has prepared some sort of special treat for us. Perhaps you'd like to get it, my dear, before we start?"

The wizard watched Princess Teddy leave the room with the slightly bowlegged walk of someone who'd spent the day in the saddle.

The king shook his head and looked out the window.

"We've tried. Heaven knows, we've tried," the queen said. "But she does not look like a princess, she does not act like a princess…"

"Well…," said the wizard only to fill the silence, but he found himself the object of two expectant stares. He cleared his throat and tapped his fingers on his knees. He looked out the window. "It's not that she's unattractive—"

"Princesses are supposed to be exquisite," the king said. "They're supposed to have unsurpassed beauty—beauty to leave young men breathless with admiration. They are *not* supposed to have freckles, and they are *not* supposed to bite their fingernails, and they are *definitely not* supposed to loom over prospective suitors like a…a…"

"Like an older sister," the queen said, "who's better at riding, and archery, and tracking in the woods…" She was counting these things off on her fingers.

"And who won't give in during an argument—"

"And *doesn't have time* to learn how to do lady-like things such as embroidery and cooking—"

"Here we go!" Teddy burst into the room, using her foot both to push open the door and to shut it behind her. She placed the dish she was carrying on the short table before them. "Baking is not my strong point," she explained to the wizard, "but Mother insisted that I whip up something special because you were coming."

The wizard stared at the red-white-and-green mound of crumbs on the platter before him. The thought that came to his mind was *Pastry Attacked by Demented Baker*.

"I had a little bit of trouble getting it out of the pan," she explained when the three of them didn't move and only sat there staring. Finally, she explained, "It's peppermint cake, with pistachio icing."

The queen pulled a lacy handkerchief from her sleeve and leaned back on the sofa, covering her mouth.

The king gulped down the last of his cold tea and looked away.

The princess slid a piece of the cake onto a silver plate and handed it to the wizard. "I suppose they've told you they're having no luck in marrying me off."

"Really, my dear," the queen said from behind her handkerchief.

"No, it's quite all right. I understand. Princes come to visit, but we never hit it off well. I always think they're young and silly, and they always suddenly remember urgent business elsewhere. Mother and Father are frantic. Here I am, their only child, the heir apparent to one of the nicest realms in the area, and I haven't had a

★ Wizard at Work ★

single offer. My friends are all married already. The *younger sisters* of my friends are all married already. I've become an embarrassment." Teddy sat on the floor, cross-legged, and leaned her elbows on the coffee table, her chin on her hands. "So. What's the plan?"

The wizard avoided her steady gaze. He concentrated, instead, on his cake. He tried to hide the fact that his fork was unable to put a dent in it. "Well...," he said.

"Can you work some sort of spell to improve my looks? To make me less..." She gestured helplessly. "...less like me and more like what a princess should be?"

The wizard bore down on his fork, and a piece of cake broke away and skittered off the plate, hitting his teacup with a loud *ping!*

Princess Teddy stared at the cup. "Know any nearsighted princes," she asked softly, "who are on diets?"

"Now look here." The wizard put his fork down emphatically. He looked from princess, to king, to queen, back to princess. "You are a perfectly fine princess as you are." He held up a finger so no one would interrupt. "All we need here is just a little something extra. A sense of mystery! Adventure! Quest! A prize hard-won!"

"I beg your pardon?" the queen asked.

"A test?" Teddy said. "Are you talking about some sort of test?"

"Exactly." The wizard stood up and began to pace the room. "We'll announce that only the man who can pass the test will be worthy of the princess's hand. Once we whip up their competitive spirit—"

"Ah, yes, I can see it!" the princess interrupted. "We'll have the next poor fool who wanders into the kingdom perform some incredible feat, like touch his toes twice or balance a book on his head for seven seconds, or maybe we can pose him a riddle, like asking what's his name and where he's from—and if he answers correctly, then he's got to marry me."

"Well," agreed the king, "more or less."

"No," the wizard said firmly. Then he repeated it for emphasis. "No." He looked directly at the princess. "That would be demeaning."

Now she looked away.

"Trust me. All you need to do is generate a little enthusiasm. You don't need to resort to trickery."

She ran her hand through her hair, trying to force it into some sort of manageability. "All right," she said softly. "I agree. I will marry the man who can pass the test you devise. Now, what shall it be?"

The wizard was struck by inspiration. "We will ask the suitors to present you with three golden cucumbers from the secret garden of the dwarf Maximilian. That way, if you don't like a particular suitor—if he's too young, or too silly, or too whatever—all you have to do is refuse to accept the cucumbers from him, and the quest isn't considered fulfilled."

"Cucumbers?" the king said. "*Cucumbers? Isn't one usually sent in quest of golden apples?*"

"Anybody can do apples," the wizard scoffed.

"Oh, well, thank you very much!" Teddy said. "But I've heard about this dwarf Maximilian. Funeral arrangements to be handled by the family. Calling hours, eight to ten. No flowers, please."

"Now, see here," the wizard said. "It's hard, but not impossible."

" 'Not impossible,' " Teddy repeated. "Maybe not for a wizard." She started biting one of her fingernails.

"Really," he assured her. Then, ignoring the little voice inside his head that warned he was about to go too far, he said, "Look. I'll prove it can be done. *I'll* do it."

"Without magic?" Teddy asked.

The wizard nodded, but she continued to look worried. It wasn't fair, he thought. After seeing how princesses like Rosalie and Gilbertina could attract royal suitors, the wizard felt it just wasn't fair that a sweet girl like Teddy couldn't, if that was what she wanted. His sense of outrage prompted him to say, "Well, my goodness, if you don't trust me, if you want to come along to check up on me—"

"Oh," she said. "What a fine idea! Thank you."

The king leaped to his feet to shake the wizard's hand.

"Well, that's settled then." The queen stood up and smiled. "Have a nice trip."

The wizard took a deep breath and wondered how he got himself into these things. Maybe he could blame this on that witch he'd met in the blacksmith's shop—the one who may or may not have cursed him.

He was to wonder about that many times in the three days it took to reach the island ruled by the dwarf king Maximilian.

They had to travel by horse, for Princess Teddy insisted that even the wizard's transporting spell, being magic, was not fair.

"But there's nothing here," the wizard complained as their horses plodded along the dusty trail, which caused him to alternately cough and sneeze. "There's just plains and meadows and small towns until we get to Maximilian's lake: no danger, nothing interesting."

"Still, you never know," Teddy kept saying.

So they rode, and they camped out, and the wizard volunteered to do all the cooking. Still, the time passed quickly, for Teddy was good company and knew or made up all sorts of exciting stories.

After three days had passed, quicker than the wizard would have thought possible, they came to the edge of the lake that surrounded the dwarf king's forbidden island.

Princess Teddy looked from the dwarf king's walled garden, which they could see from the far shore, to the water that separated them from it. "What kind of fish are those?" she asked apprehensively, pointing at the large, dark shapes that watched them from the water.

The wizard studied them warily. "I don't know, but they certainly have a lot of teeth, don't they?"

Teddy pulled him back from the edge. "Careful. That one was licking its lips when you leaned over like that."

The wizard didn't think fish—even hungry fish—licked their lips, but he decided to keep his distance, just in case. He said, "Dwarfs are nothing if not practical. And casting a spell each time they come here from their kingdom beneath the mountain would be an awful waste of magic. So we can assume there's a nonmagical way to cross." He began walking along the edge, peering at the water. The shadowy creatures in the lake stared back at him.

"Ways to cross a body of water," Teddy said, and began to count on her fingers. "Boat: We don't have one. Swim: We don't dare. Jump: We couldn't. Bridge: We don't see one…"

The wizard grabbed the finger she had used for the last point. "Exactly!"

"Exactly what?"

"There has to be a bridge," the wizard said, "but we can't see it. Why? What can you see right through?"

Teddy bit at a fingernail. "Air…water…" She studied his face for a change of expression. "Glass…"

He grinned and pointed to the water directly in front of them. To the left, a school of nasty little fish with long sharp teeth waited expectantly. To the right hovered a nasty big fish—which also had long sharp teeth. But in front of them there was a span of water that none of the creatures crossed. There was no visible boundary in the water, and the sandy bottom of the lake stretched unmarked to either side, yet for as long as the two of them looked, nothing passed through it.

"A glass bridge," Teddy whispered, "just below the surface of the water."

The wizard led the way, but Teddy followed close after. The glass bridge was narrow and slippery, and the lake creatures, big and little, swam as close to it as they could. The wizard could almost believe that he heard them grinding their teeth in frustration, but that was as silly as the picture of them licking their hungry fish lips. He and the princess made it safely to the other side.

"Whew!" she said. Then she gasped. "Look out!"

A dwarf had leaped over the wall that surrounded the garden and was now running down the hill toward them.

"I thought you said the dwarfs lived in a kingdom under the mountain," Teddy said. She took a step back as the little man approached, holding on to his crown with one hand and waving an ax with the other. "Why is their king guarding their garden?"

The wizard was confused. "He shouldn't be here. King Maximilian and his people *do* live under the mountain. Surely he's got more important things to do than sit here day after day protecting the vegetation."

But even as the wizard spoke, the dwarf king came to a stop just a few feet from them. Though he was short, he had very muscular arms, and his face was one even a mother would call nasty. He straightened his crown and said in a voice that was almost as much whine as growl: "You've come for my cucumbers, haven't you? Everybody always tries to steal my cucumbers. Two knights can't agree who's the best, they decide the one who can steal Maximilian's cucumbers is the winner. Prince wants to prove he's worthy of some lady's love, he steals a cucumber from poor Maximilian. Father doesn't have a dowry for his daughter, he sneaks in here, 'cause old Maximilian can be counted on to have enough gold for a hundred dowries, if you don't mind it coming in a vegetable state. I bet you have some long, sad, perfectly reasonable reason to be here, too, don't you?"

With a guilty expression, Teddy glanced at the wizard. "Well, I—"

"Ha!" Maximilian snorted. "A likely story!"

The wizard put his hand in front of his mouth and cleared his throat, then left his hand blocking his mouth to whisper to Teddy, "He shouldn't be here."

"You should be *ashamed* of yourselves," the dwarf king said, once again whining, "tall people like you." He held his ax higher, threatening.

Still, the wizard shook his head. "King Maximilian *here*? To guard a few golden cucumbers?"

Teddy leaned close to whisper into his ear, "This is not all that important, you know."

"Of course it is," he told her, though Maximilian had taken a step closer. The wizard gave Teddy what he hoped was a reassuring smile. He said to her, "I told you, dwarfs are practical. I think Maximilian's too practical to sit here day after day on the off chance that someone makes it past the lake. This figure is only imaginary. A spirit guard." More quietly, he added, "I hope." He found himself holding Princess Teddy's hand. Even her freckles had turned pale, but he was impressed that she had neither fainted—something princesses were distressingly prone to do—nor tried to run away. "We see him, but he does not exist," the wizard insisted, partly for her benefit but also to reassure himself.

"Last chance to run away," Maximilian warned.

The wizard and Teddy stood fast.

The dwarf swung the ax.

The wizard could see the hairs in the little warrior's warts, and he could feel the rush of air from the ax, swinging to chop off his head.

129

But the ax passed right through him, so that the wizard couldn't even feel it, but only saw the blade again as it passed out through the other side.

The wizard closed his eyes and mentally counted to ten before he could breathe normally again. Then he walked through the image of Maximilian, who continued to swing his ax as though hewing his way through an army of wizards.

Sighing with relief, Princess Teddy pulled her frizzy brown hair away from her face and followed the wizard. Maximilian stayed on the bank, still hacking away with his ax. "Now what?" Teddy asked.

"Now," the wizard said, once his voice had come back, "we get the cucumbers."

But that was easier said than done. There were pear trees and peach trees and cherry trees, and all sorts of nut trees. There were grapevines, berry bushes, tomato plants, and cornstalks. (The wizard really envied the dwarf's garden.) But there was no vine with golden cucumbers.

"I don't understand it," the wizard said.

There was, in fact, only one cucumber vine in

the entire garden. It grew up and around a lattice arch, and the two travelers stood beneath it, looking up at the multitude of large, very ordinary, very green cucumbers.

"Maybe golden cucumbers are green until they get ripe," Teddy suggested without much conviction.

"Maybe," the wizard said, trying to sound more hopeful than he felt, for some of the cucumbers looked perfectly ripe to him, but there wasn't a hint of gold. "Or maybe the gold ones grow on the same vine as the regular ones, and they're hidden under the leaves."

"Maybe," Teddy agreed, but the wizard suspected she said that only to be polite.

The wizard climbed up the trellis, but after a few minutes he was all sweaty, and he had twigs and leaves caught in his hair and scratches on his arms. "That does it," he said, jumping back down to the ground. "You were right: It can't be done. We'll think of another quest to test your prospective suitors."

"You know," said Teddy, "I was just thinking.

First, we came to something that we couldn't see but that was there: the glass bridge. Then we came to something that we *could* see but that wasn't really there: the guardian dwarf." She circled the trellis thoughtfully. "Now here we've got something that we can see, which presumably is really here, but which, perhaps…"

"…*isn't* what it seems to be," the wizard finished. He nodded. "Very good. Very, very good. I'm impressed."

Princess Teddy blushed. "Well, before you get too impressed, check to see if I'm right."

The wizard reached up and put a hand around one of the plump green cucumbers. He tugged it loose, and felt it grow warm and heavy in his hand. He lowered his arm, held the cucumber out before them, and was surprised that his hand shook a bit. The sun sparkled on the cucumber's smooth surface as it slowly turned to solid gold, shiny enough for him to see his bedraggled reflection. He took a deep breath and looked at the princess's face. He'd done it. He'd proved that someone—without using magic—could get the golden cucumbers. If he could do it, so could someone else, and that someone would marry Princess Teddy. The wizard's job was done. So why was he feeling so sad? He held the cucumber out to Teddy.

She made a small move as though to take it from him, then pulled back her hand. "You said three," she murmured—though, being taller, she could have reached them better than he.

The wizard plucked two more, then held all three out to her. "See," he said with a bow, "it is possible for a man to steal three of the golden cucumbers from the secret garden of the dwarf Maximilian, *without magic*, and win the hand of the princess Theodora."

She accepted the cucumbers with a shy smile, then said, "Gotcha!"

The wizard's smile vanished. "I beg your pardon?"

"Gotcha. And you know it: You filled every requirement of the quest." She pointed a finger with a ragged fingernail. "Right?"

"Now wait a moment—"

"Right?"

The wizard sighed, folded his arms across his chest, and sighed again. The princess was watching him with an anxious expression. But he didn't notice her frizzy hair, or her freckles, or the fact that he had to tilt his head back to look her in the eye; he thought of the funny stories she had told to pass the time on their trip, and of her cleverness and her bravery. She was, he thought, the most exquisitely beautiful princess he'd ever met. The witch had been perfectly right about true happiness. He shook his head, but he smiled as he did so. "Got me," he admitted.

Teddy looked away. "Not that I'd really force you—"

The wizard took her hand and kissed it gently. "Let's go home," he said, "my princess."

And they did.